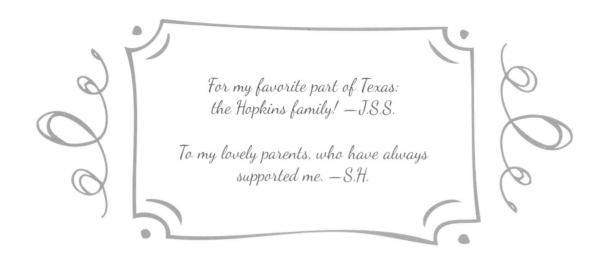

For my favorite part of Texas:
the Hopkins family! —J.S.S.

To my lovely parents, who have always
supported me. —S.H.

Published by Familius™ LLC, www.familius.com

Familius books are available at special discounts for bulk purchases, whether for sales promotions
or for family or corporate use. For more information, contact Premium Sales at 559-876-2170 or
email orders@familius.com.

Library of Congress Cataloging-in-Publication Data
2016942210   ISBN 9781942934035

Printed in China

Book and jacket design by David Miles
Edited by Lindsay Sandberg and Erika Riggs

10 9 8 7 6 5 4 3 2 1

First Edition

12 Little Elves visit TEXAS

BY JESS SMART SMILEY

ILLUSTRATIONS BY SADIE HAN

FAMILIUS

’Twas Christmas in Texas,
and twelve elves were sent
to see who was sleeping . . .

away the elves went!

In each home was nestled each girl and each boy,

while visions of Texas brought everyone joy.

The Alamo glistened
with lights and pine trees,
as the carolers' tunes
danced on the breeze.

FORT WORTH

The stockyards in Fort Worth
had bulls and cowboys,
broncos and lassos, and rodeo toys.

STOCK YARDS

Big Tex welcomed all to the Texas State Fair,
where barbecue tang filled up the air.

NASA prepared to send crews into space
while mission control decorated the place!

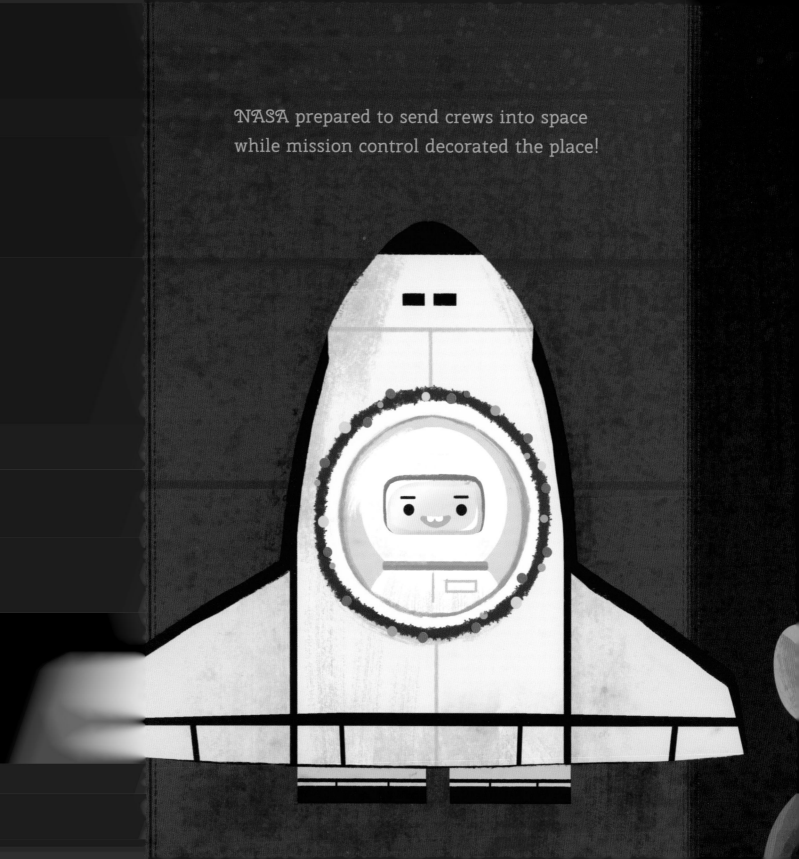

In Austin, the capitol
sparkled and gleamed.

The twelve elves continued,
while each Texan dreamed . . .

TOUCHDOWN!

. . . of touchdowns and tackles
that lit the scoreboard.
Each fan stood and cheered
when Santa Claus scored!

At the Cadillac Ranch,
the cars were all jolly.
Painted bright red and green,
they looked like fresh holly.

The Riverwalk in
San Antonio glowed
with tinsel and bright lights
and ribbons and bows.

Out in the country
in the quiet of night,
coyotes in Big Bend
howled in the moonlight.

Adios, dear Texas.
You're all fast asleep,
but there's just one more house
that the elves want to see . . .

Y'all hurry to bed now
and shut your eyes tight.
Merry Christmas, dear Texas.
Twelve elves say goodnight!